To Molly, *Secretary of Design*

Madam PRESIDENT

LANE SMITH

HYPERION BOOKS FOR CHILDREN NEW YORK

AN IMPRINT OF DISNEY BOOK GROUP

A president has many duties.

There are executive orders to give,

daily briefs to review,

one lunch to approve,

photo ops to be shot,

babies to kiss,

treaties to negotiate,

and state funerals to attend.

A president must choose a capable cabinet.

Secretary of
the Treasury

Secretary
of State

Secretary of
Agriculture

Secretary of
Education

Secretary
of Soccer

Secretary
of Naps

Secretary of
Pets Who
Should Be
in Their
Cages

Secretary of
Transportation

Secretary of
the Interior

Secretary
of Fantasy

Secretary
of Pizza

Secretary
of Defense

Soldier

Secretary
of Energy

Secretary of
Undersea
Exploration

Secretary
of Dance

Secretary
of Health

Secretary of
Secretaries

A president is important:
Commander in Chief,

Head of State,

Fearless Leader,

Chief Executive,

Head Honcho,

Big Cheese!

WHY, THE PRESIDENT IS THE MOST IMPORTANT PERSON IN THE WHOLE WIDE WORLD!

And the most humble.

A president must be protected at all times.

A president must be a diplomat . . .

which is why I'm not commenting on that hat.

A president has her own theme song.

Hail to the Chief

Hail to the chief we have cho-sen for the na-tion,

Hail to the chief! The most awe-some one of all.——

Hail to the chief and her rad ad-min-i-stra-tion,

Hail to the chief from the moun-tain to the mall.

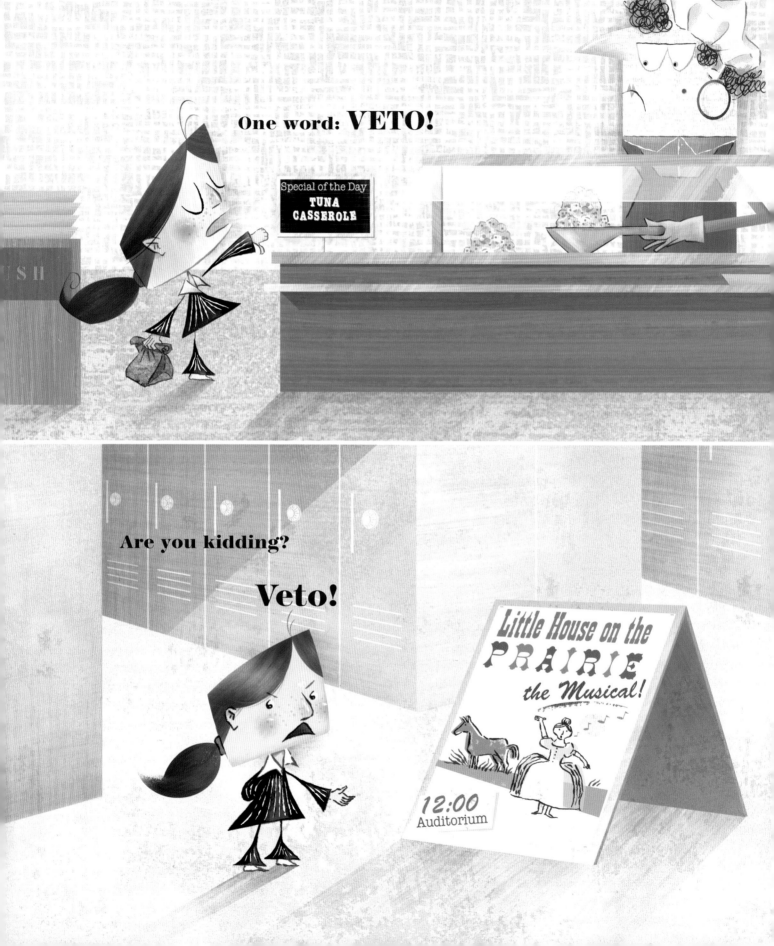

A president must tackle
press conferences gracefully.

ORAL REPORTS TODAY!

SEAL OF THE PRESIDENT OF THE UNITED STATES

That's top secret.
No comment.
I'll get back to you on that.
I won't dignify that question with a response.
C'mon, Tiffany, get real!
No comment.
Let me think about that.
I know you are, but what am I?
Next question.
No comment!

THE MOON   THE EARTH

THE MOON   THE EARTH

THE MOON   THE EARTH

A president must keep the peace.

Even at day's end, a president's work is never done.

A disaster. WOW!

**A president must show she
can keep her head in a crisis.**

**Oh my. It's much worse than I thought.
A Disaster Area if ever I saw one!**

A president has to lead by example, even if it means cleaning her own room.

Disaster contained. The nation is at rest.

What's that?

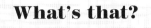

The ambassador from Freedonia is here?

He can see the vice president.

Sometimes even a president gets pooped.

DESIGN BY MOLLY LEACH

All rights reserved. Published by Hyperion Books for Children, an imprint of Disney Book Group. No part of this book may be reproduced or transmitted in any form or by any means, electronic or mechanical, including photocopying, recording, or by any information storage and retrieval system, without written permission from the publisher. For information address Hyperion Books for Children, 114 Fifth Avenue, New York, New York 10011-5690.

Printed in Hong Kong
First Edition
1 3 5 7 9 10 8 6 4 2
Library of Congress Cataloging-in-Publication Data on file.
ISBN-13: 978-1-4231-0846-7
ISBN-10: 1-4231-0846-9

Reinforced binding
Visit www.hyperionbooksforchildren.com

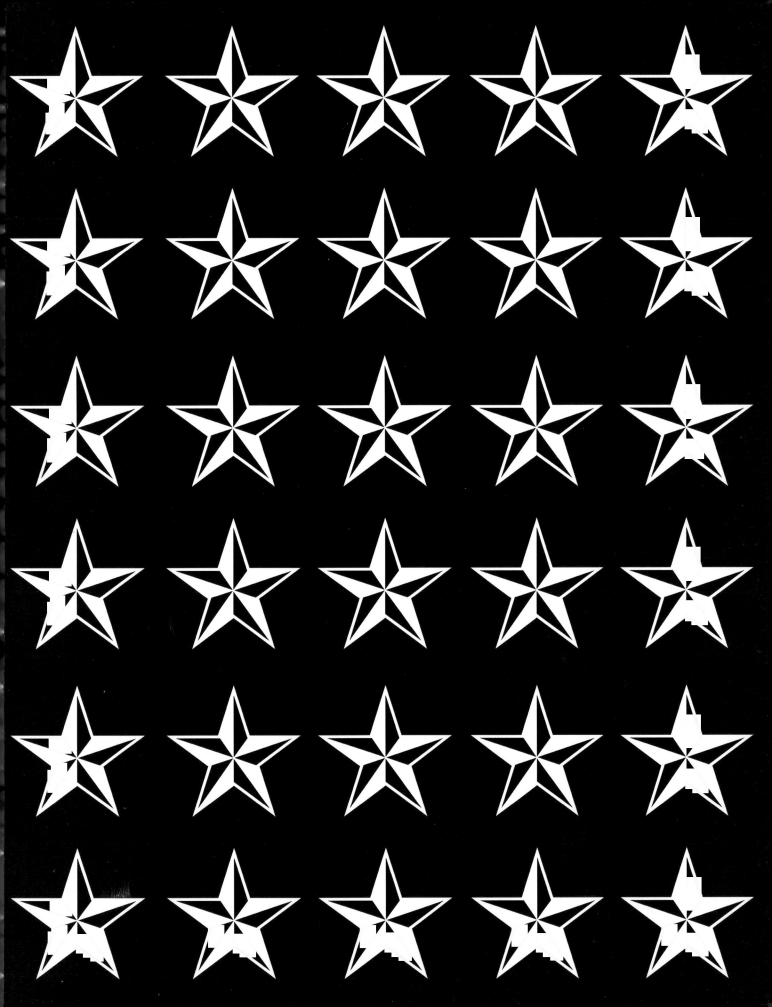